Be Afraid—Be Very Afraid

Look out for more books in the Goosebumps Series 2000
by R.L. Stine:

And coming soon:

Be Afraid—Be Very Afraid

R.L. Stine

Hippo

Scholastic Children's Books
Commonwealth House, 1–19 New Oxford Street, London WC1A 1NU, UK
a division of Scholastic Ltd
London ~ New York ~ Toronto ~ Sydney ~ Auckland
Mexico City ~ New Delhi ~ Hong Kong

First published in the USA by Scholastic Inc., 1999
First published in the UK by Scholastic Ltd, 2000

ISBN 0 439 01335 6

Typeset by Rowland Phototypesetting Ltd, Bury St Edmunds, Suffolk
Printed by Mackays of Chatham plc, Chatham, Kent.

10 9 8 7 6 5 4 3 2 1

My name is Connor Buckley, and I am the King of Evil.

Well, no. I'm not *really* the King of Evil. That's the character I decided to play in the card game.

What card game?

I'll get to that later. But let me tell you this—once you choose a character, you're stuck with it. You have to be that character every time you play the game.

Then, every card you pick, every roll of the dice, means something important to your character...

Unless you die.

My friends and I had never tried any role-playing games. But as soon as we opened the box of cards and began to check them out, we were hooked.

We had no idea how *real* the game could become.

1

Or how dangerous.

I'd better start at the beginning. My friend Emily Zinman always tells me to slow down. "Cool your jets, Connor." That's what she says. "Take a deep breath. Count to ten. Try some decaf."

Decaf? I don't drink coffee. I'm twelve years old! Coffee tastes like bitter *mud* to me!

I can't help it. I have a lot of energy. I know I can't keep still. I'm always bouncing off the walls, talking a mile a minute, dancing, hopping, bopping.

So, what's the problem? Can I help it if other people are slooooooow?

It was nearly the end of summer, and Emily and I were bored.

Long, hot days with nothing to do. Only a couple of weeks until school started.

We had read all of our summer reading books. We had played every computer game we own a thousand times. We had survived our family holidays with only a few dozen mosquito bites. We swam, played tennis, hung out with friends, laughing and doing nothing.

And now we were totally bored.

We were sitting under the split maple tree in my front garden. Actually, Emily was perched in the split part of the trunk.

You see, the tree was hit by lightning last year and had split right down the middle. Half

2

the trunk bent one way. The other half bent the other. It looks like twin arches.

Most people would probably have the tree dug up and carried away. But my parents are weird. Actually, they're architects. They design houses. They're very artistic.

They thought the split tree looked like a piece of sculpture. So they kept it. It's actually great for sitting on and climbing.

But Emily and I had been sitting on it and climbing it all summer, and we were borrrrrrred.

Did I mention that we were bored?

I was sitting on the ground in the shade of the tree, pulling up clumps of grass and throwing them at Emily. Yes, I know it's not right to rip up the grass. But I can't just sit there. I have to keep my hands busy.

The back of my neck started to itch. I reached back and pulled off a big black ant.

From her perch in the tree, Emily laughed. I guessed that she had plucked the ant off the tree trunk and dropped it down my shirt.

"Give me a break," I muttered.

"Make me," she replied.

We were so bored, we were turning stupid.

"Maybe I'll go home and streak my hair," she sighed.

I threw another clump of grass at her. "Your hair is already streaked," I said. She had come

3

back from holiday with light blonde streaks through her brown hair.

"Maybe I'll streak it some more," she said. "I need a new look for when school starts."

"You need a new face!" I told her.

She didn't laugh. She never laughs at my jokes. But I keep trying.

"Hey—what's going on over there?" she asked, jumping down from the tree. She brushed off the back of her white tennis shorts and stepped beside me.

I jumped to my feet and gazed down the block. A group of people were gathered at the house on the next corner. "Looks like a garage sale," I said, pulling a twig off Emily's shoulder.

"At Mr Zarwid's house? Weird!" Emily exclaimed.

Yes, it was definitely weird. Mr Zarwid is the neighbourhood grouch. He isn't friendly to anyone, and he hates kids.

Last autumn, I knocked on the front door of his creepy old house and tried to sell him some sweets for our school fund-raiser. He sent his big Alsatian after me.

I'm a fast runner—but I set Olympic *records* that day!

What could weird old Mr Zarwid be selling? I wondered. I started half running, half skipping down the driveway. "Let's check it out!"

Emily stayed back. "I—I don't like that man. He was really nasty to my sisters. He—"

"Let's just see what he's selling," I called back to her. I was already halfway down the block. "It's probably torture racks and bullwhips and chain-saws!" I joked.

Emily didn't laugh.

As we made our way across Mr Zarwid's neatly trimmed front garden, we saw four or five neighbours in front of the open garage. They were pawing over items for sale.

Not bullwhips and chain-saws. The usual garage-sale things. I stepped up to the first table and saw a stack of old hunting-and-fishing magazines, a shiny pair of old-fashioned-looking shoes, dented binoculars, an ashtray shaped like an ocean shell.

Bor-rrring.

"How much is this?" A woman held up an oil painting in a fancy gold frame. It showed a sailing-boat in a purple sunset.

"Twenty," Mr Zarwid called. He sat on a folding chair just inside the garage, leaning back with his thin yellow arms folded behind his head.

He has wavy white hair parted in the middle and a white moustache that's really weird. It stands out straight from both sides of his square red face. I've never seen a moustache do that.

But it's his eyes that really give me the creeps.

His mean little blue eyes always seem to be glaring angrily. He scowls and mutters to himself a lot too.

He was wearing baggy, stained khaki shorts and a sleeveless red T-shirt that just barely covered his big belly. I could see tufts of white hair on his chest.

The woman leaned the painting against the table.

"If you break it, you take it," Mr Zarwid called in his scratchy, high voice. Then he cackled to himself, his white moustache bobbing up and down.

Emily flipped through an old book of nursery rhymes. "Let's go," she whispered, giving me a push towards the street. "This is all *junk*."

A table half hidden inside the garage caught my eye. It seemed to have dozens of small statues on it. Ignoring Emily, I jogged round a rack of old coats into the garage.

I stepped over to the cluttered table to examine the figures. They weren't statues, I discovered. They were candlesticks. I saw dragons and elves and strange animals and monsters carved out of dark wood.

I picked one up to study. It appeared to be half man, half horse.

Emily stepped beside me. "Gross," she muttered. "Check this one out." She raised a fat creature with a long rat's tail.

"That one looks like you!" I joked. "Before you streaked your hair."

Emily didn't laugh.

"Hey, you kids," I heard Mr Zarwid rasp. "What are you trying to steal?"

He climbed to his feet and stood staring at us with those mean blue eyes, scowling angrily, hands on his hips.

Emily dropped the carved candlestick on the table. "We—we're not stealing anything," she stammered.

"We're just looking," I added.

"This stuff isn't for kids," the old man growled. "Maybe you should go home and play with your teddy bears."

Teddy bears?

I could see everyone staring at Emily and me. My face felt hot. I knew I was blushing.

"We weren't doing anything!" I protested.

"I've seen you young hoodlums before," Mr Zarwid replied.

Hoodlums?

He didn't move. He was staring us down, his cold blue eyes moving from Emily to me.

"Let's go," Emily murmured. "He's . . . crazy."

I followed her out of the garage. We brushed past two women from the neighbourhood who were staring at us accusingly. Squeezed through a row of cluttered tables, loaded down with junk.

Then we both took off running.

I didn't look back. We didn't stop until we got to my back garden. I pulled open the kitchen door and we hurried inside.

"Anyone home?" I called out breathlessly.

No. No reply.

Still breathing hard, I reached into the pocket of my shorts and threw something on to the kitchen table.

"What's that?" Emily demanded.

I grinned at her.

"Connor—what *is* that?" she repeated.

My grin grew wider. "Something I stole," I told her.

Her mouth dropped open in shock. "You *what*?"

"He had no right to accuse us," I said. "He had no right to embarrass us like that. So I got angry. And I grabbed something off a table when we ran."

Emily narrowed her eyes at me. Then she turned to the small rectangular box. "What *is* it?" she demanded. "What did you steal?"

I picked it up and threw it to her. "Think fast!"

She grabbed for it. Missed. And it sailed across the kitchen floor.

I dived under the breakfast table and picked it up off the floor. "It's a pack of cards."

She squinted at me. "Cards? What a stupid thing to steal. You don't like playing card games, remember?"

She's right. I can't sit still for card games. I get too restless.

I gazed at the box and read the words out loud: "'Be Afraid'."

Emily stared at me. "Excuse me?"

"That's the name of the card game," I told her. "Be Afraid."

"Weird," she muttered.

I opened the box and slid out the pack of cards. "Check these out," I murmured.

I flipped through them quickly. The cards all had pictures on them. Pictures of masked knights, evil-looking dwarves, dragons, husky little guys with pig faces.

"Awesome graphics," I said.

"Connor, these cards look really old," Emily replied. "Maybe they're valuable. Maybe you should return them."

I opened my mouth to reply. But before I could utter a sound, a nearby voice boomed, *"Prepare to die!"*

I cried out, startled, and the cards fell from my hand. They scattered over the floor.

As I bent to pick them up, the kitchen door swung open. "Prepare to die!" our friend Kyle Boots repeated, stomping heavily into the kitchen.

Kyle is big and blond and powerful-looking, and he likes scaring people. He plays tackle on our junior high football team. But he's as big as some of the high school players.

Kyle's claim to fame is that his voice changed when he was eleven. He loves showing off his deep, deep voice—especially round the rest of us, who still sound like kids. When he booms out "Prepare to die!" it's pretty awesome.

"What's up, guys?" he demanded, gazing down at me. "What are you doing down there, Connor? Looking for crumbs?"

"Huh? Crumbs?" I gathered up the last of the cards. "Why would I be looking for crumbs?"

"That's what my dog does," Kyle replied.

I climbed to my feet. "I'm not your dog."

"I know," Kyle replied. "I can tell the difference. My dog is smart."

Emily laughed at that.

What is her problem?

"Check these out," I said, shoving the cards towards Kyle.

"Connor stole a pack of weird cards," Emily reported.

Kyle squinted at me. "You *stole* them?" He glanced at the box on the table. "Oh. Be Afraid. Yeah, sure. I know that game."

"You know it?" I asked.

He nodded, his blond hair falling over his broad forehead. "Yeah. I've played it with some older guys." He brushed the hair back with his big hand.

"How do you play?" Emily asked.

"It's a role-playing game," Kyle explained. "You know. Evil kings and knights and dragons and stuff. Lots of battles. Magic. Sorcery. There are hundreds of different packs. Kids collect them."

He grabbed the cards from my hand. "Let's see which one you've got."

He turned the cards over, raised them close to his face, and began to shuffle through them slowly.

Suddenly, he stopped and stared at one of the cards. Stared until his eyes bulged.

"Oh, no!" Kyle cried in horror. "No! I don't believe it!"

I felt my heart skip a beat. "Kyle—what?" I cried. "What's wrong?"

A smile slowly spread across his beefy face. His brown eyes flashed merrily. "Gotcha," he whispered.

Emily tossed back her head and laughed again.

Why does she think Kyle is such a riot?

Kyle crossed the room to the refrigerator. He opened the door, searched the shelves, and pulled out a can of Coke.

"Help yourself," I muttered.

He had already opened the top and tilted the can over his open mouth. He let the Coke pour down his throat, gulping noisily, until he'd emptied the can. Then he burped long and loud and threw the can on the worktop.

"Let's try the game," he suggested. He dropped into a chair at the kitchen table and began shuffling through the Be Afraid cards.

Emily sat down opposite him with her back to the kitchen window. Late afternoon sunlight poured through the window, making both of them glow.

"Connor, go and get some dice," Kyle ordered. "We need at least four. Have you got them?"

"I think so," I replied. "I'll go and see."

I ran to the den, where we keep all the board games. I tore open the boxes and searched until I found four dice.

When I returned to the kitchen, Kyle had divided the pack into four neat stacks. The cards were all face down.

I dropped the dice on to the table and took a seat. "How do we play?" I asked Kyle.

"I've divided the pack into four piles," he explained, tapping each stack with his finger. "Character cards, Power cards, Action cards and Fate cards. First you have to choose the character you are going to play."

He shoved one of the piles of cards across the table to me. "Pick a Character card. From anywhere in the pile."

I picked up the cards and pulled one from the middle. I turned it over and studied it. "King!" I declared. "Hey—that's cool. I'm a king!"

"That's not fair," Emily protested. "Why did Connor go first? We should roll the dice for it or something. Why should he be king?"

"Since I've played before, I'll make the rules,"

Kyle told Emily, shoving the stack of cards towards her. "It's a very complicated game. It takes months to learn."

"But if Connor is king—" Emily started.

"Being king is no big deal," Kyle interrupted. "He might be a really *weak* king. He might be a total loser. We haven't drawn our Power cards yet."

Kyle grinned. "Connor might be a powerless king. Maybe even a helpless slave to one of us!"

"Yeah. That's what I want to be," Emily said. "Someone more powerful than the king."

"In your dreams," I muttered. "As soon as we start, I'm going to have both of your heads cut off!"

Emily frowned across the table at me. "That's mean, Connor," she said softly.

"Just pick a character," Kyle sighed. "Any time this year."

Emily shut her eyes and picked a Character card. She studied it. "A Goth? Yuck. What's a Goth?" she cried, unable to hide her disappointment.

Kyle took the card from her. "A Goth is a mutant sorcerer," he told her.

Emily brightened a little. "A sorcerer? You mean I have magical powers?"

"Maybe," Kyle replied.

Emily turned to me. "Maybe I'll turn the king into a frog," she threatened.

I replied with some croaking sounds. I do a really good frog imitation. Very loud and very realistic. Ask anyone.

Kyle slammed the table with his fist. All the cards bounced. "Come on, guys," he pleaded. "Let's take the game seriously."

I stopped my frog sounds. When Kyle wants people to be serious, they'd better get serious.

Kyle shuffled the Character cards. Then he picked one. "I'm a Krel," he announced.

He showed us the card. It had a painting of an ugly dwarf-creature with pink pointed ears and an animal snout. The Krel wore a furry red hat and carried a curved dagger.

"What exactly is a Krel?" I asked. "Is it good or bad?"

"Depends," Kyle answered.

"Is a Goth more powerful than a Krel?" Emily asked.

"Depends," Kyle replied again.

He shoved the dice towards me. "Now we're going to roll for power points. Go ahead. Roll all four dice. Now we'll see what's what. You get a hundred power points for every point on the dice."

We took turns rolling the dice. I rolled all fives and sixes. "Yaaay!" I cried. "Power! I've got the power!"

Emily and Kyle both rolled twos and threes.

"The king is very powerful," Kyle announced

solemnly. He turned to Emily. "You and I will have to work together, or we don't stand a chance."

I jumped up, pumped my fists above my head, and let out a cheer. "The king rules!" I cried.

"We'll see about that," Kyle growled.

"Sit down, Connor," Emily ordered.

"It's *King* Connor," I corrected her. But I dropped back into my chair.

"Let's get started," Kyle said. "The game is like an ancient story. Shut your eyes. Pretend we're in ancient times. We live in a forest. At the edge of the forest stands a tall castle."

"*My* castle!" I interrupted.

Kyle ignored me. He lowered his voice to a deep whisper. "The forest is filled with all kinds of danger. Strange creatures. Masked knights. Mutant invaders. Krels and Goths and Mords and Jekels. Strange animals, poisonous plants, evil enemies lurking everywhere."

He slid a stack of cards in front of me. "Start the action, King. Pick the top card and turn it over. Then prepare yourself for whatever comes."

Whatever comes?

Something about Kyle's solemn expression, his deep voice, his serious, dark eyes—sent a chill down my back.

I pulled the top card off the pack and turned it over.

16

It showed a fat yellow lightning bolt.

I set the card on the table.

And as I did, I heard a loud *crackle*.

And saw a bright yellow bolt of lightning through the kitchen window.

"Whoa!" I cried out.

It was bright sunshine out there. Where did the lightning come from?

I grabbed the card.

Another crackling sound. Another flash of lightning.

And in the jagged bolt of light, I saw a face—an ugly, evil, twisted face, green in the eerie glow—pressing against the window, glaring in at us.

I let out a cry and jumped up. My chair toppled over backwards and clattered to the kitchen floor.

Thunder boomed outside the window. Very close. I could hear the sound bounce off the house. The lightning flickered. And in its fading glow, I recognized the face.

Mr Zarwid! He pressed close to the window, his tiny, round eyes peering in at us. Then he motioned with one hand towards the kitchen door.

I took a deep breath and made my way to the door. "What is *he* doing here?" I cried.

As I pulled open the door, another roar of thunder shook the house. Rain pattered on the back doorstep. The old trees in the garden bent and groaned in the gusting wind.

How did the weather change so fast?

Hunching in the rain, his white hair slicked down over his forehead, Mr Zarwid climbed on to the back steps.

He had pulled a yellow raincoat over his sleeveless T-shirt and shorts. Droplets of rain glistened on the coat. He narrowed his eyes at me.

"I *thought* one of you lived here," he said in his scratchy, thin voice. His moustache moved wetly over his lip.

He gazed over my shoulder at Kyle and Emily. Emily stood up from the table and made her way beside me.

"I saw you at my garage sale," Mr Zarwid said, eyeing us both suspiciously. "A pack of cards is missing." He cleared his throat. His tiny eyes moved from Emily to me. "You don't know anything about it—do you?"

I saw Emily nod. She opened her mouth to confess. I could see she was going to tell the truth.

"No, we don't," I quickly interrupted. "We don't know anything about it."

Mr Zarwid tilted his head slightly, still studying us. "Are you sure?"

"Of course, we're sure," I replied. "We didn't steal your cards. We don't steal, Mr Zarwid."

He nodded, rubbing his chin. The rain started to come down harder. Rain dripped from the raincoat on to the kitchen floor.

He leaned into the house. Leaned towards Emily and me. Leaned very close, so close we could smell peppermint on his breath.

"I hope you're telling the truth," he said softly, through gritted teeth. "Because the cards ... they're not a game."

I felt a shiver of fright, but I stared back at him. "What do you mean?"

"It's not a game," he repeated. "It's very dangerous."

"You—you're kidding, right?" I stammered.

"Be afraid," he whispered. "Be very afraid."

Then he swept the yellow raincoat round him, turned quickly, and vanished into the storm.

I stood frozen beside Emily for a second, his words ringing in my ears. Then I shut the kitchen door and locked it.

We turned back to Kyle, who had hidden all the cards behind him. All three of us burst out laughing.

"What a joke!" I cried. Then I did a pretty good imitation of Mr Zarwid. *Be afraid. Be very afraid.*

"Is he for real?" Kyle exclaimed. He arranged the cards back on the table. "Is he for real, or what?"

"What's the big deal?" Emily demanded. "I mean, come on. They're just cards!"

Still sniggering, I picked a card off the top of the pack.

Solid black.

I set it down on the table—and all the lights went out.

"Whoa!" I nearly fell off my chair.

"What's your problem?" Emily demanded. "It's just the storm."

"I—I don't think so," I stammered. "I picked a lightning card, and there was lightning. Now I picked a black card, and all the lights went out."

I jumped up. I fumbled for the light switch on the wall. I clicked it about a dozen times. No lights.

"Cool your jets," Emily said.

"The lights always go out when it storms," Kyle chimed in. "I don't think we should freak out."

"Let's play in the dark," Emily suggested. "That will be really cool."

I had a better idea.

I made my way into the dining room and came back with the candlesticks from the table. It took a while to find matches in the dark. But a few minutes later we leaned into the orange glow of candlelight, long shadows stretching over the kitchen table.

"Let's begin again," Kyle said in his deep, solemn voice. "Emily, draw an Action card."

Emily drew a card. She held it up to the candle glow so we could see it. It showed crossed swords under a shiny battle helmet.

"The Goth has conjured an army," Kyle said. "The king's castle is under attack. The king must go out and conquer another castle."

"How do I do that?" I asked.

Thunder boomed outside. Rain drummed against the kitchen window. The candle flames bent, flickered, then rose up straight again.

"You have to raise an army too," Kyle instructed. He shoved the four dice across the table. "You get a hundred soldier-knights for every double you roll."

I cupped the dice in my hands and shook them. "Are you making up all these rules?" I asked Kyle.

"That's how you play these games, Connor," he replied, tapping his fingers impatiently on the tabletop. "I told you—I've played this game before."

"Come on. Stop shaking them. Roll the dice," Emily groaned.

I opened my hands and sent the dice rolling across the table. Three fours and a six.

"A triple," Kyle said, leaning into the candle-light to see the dice clearly. "That gets you three hundred soldiers."

"Excellent!" I declared. "What do I do next? Do I—"

I stopped when I heard voices. Men's voices. Low laughter. A horse whinnying. Shouts.

From outside?

I turned to the window. Too dark to see out. The rain had left a curtain of water over the glass.

"Can you hear that?" I whispered.

"It's the rain pounding the trees," Emily replied. "What a storm! And it came out of nowhere."

"Roll the dice again," Kyle instructed. "You need more knights. You can't defeat a castle with only three hundred knights."

I rolled again. No doubles.

Emily laughed. "I want to cast another spell on the king."

"It's not your turn," Kyle told her.

I listened for the voices outside. But all I could hear was the roar of wind and pounding rain.

The candle flames flickered and bent. All three of us leaned over the table to see better.

I rolled the dice again. Again.

Finally, I had enough knights to attack the other castle.

"Roll all four dice," Kyle instructed. "A very

powerful king lives in that castle. More powerful than you. You have to roll at least a twenty to win his castle."

"That's too hard," I grumbled.

Emily had her eyes shut. She was motioning towards me with one hand.

"What is your problem?" I asked.

"The Goth is casting a spell on the dice," Emily replied. "You're going to roll all ones, Connor. Double snake eyes."

"You're sick," I muttered.

I shook the dice between my hands and sent them clattering on to the table.

Two sixes, a five and a four. Twenty-one!

"I did it! I smashed the other castle!" I cried, jumping up and pumping both fists in the air.

I froze when I heard the deafening crash.

All three of us cried out.

"What was that?" Emily gasped, her eyes wide with fright.

"It sounded like an explosion," Kyle murmured. "Or maybe a car crash."

I heard angry voices. Loud shouts.

High, shrill cries.

Cries of *attack*?

And then a furious clatter. Like metal clanging against metal.

Swords?

More cries and groans.

I glanced out of the window—then quickly

looked away. I really didn't want to see what was out there.

"It sounds like a battle," Emily declared in a frightened, tiny voice.

"I—I don't like this," I stammered. "I think we have to stop this game."

My hands shook as I swept them over the cards. I gathered them all up. Shoved them into a pile. Straightened them and then slid them back into the box.

I closed the box—and the lights flashed back on!

"Hey!" I choked out, blinking in the bright light.

"What's going on here?" Emily asked, hands pressed against her cheeks. "Why did the lights go back on when you closed the card box?"

"It's just a coincidence, that's all," Kyle said. "No big deal."

But Kyle froze when we heard the footsteps.

Footsteps treading down the hall. Moving towards us in the kitchen. Moving fast.

We all shrieked as an ugly dwarf-creature burst into the room.

Emily screamed. Kyle rose to his feet, fists at his sides, ready for a fight. I jumped back against the wall, my heart pounding.

The dwarf-creature threw back his big, round head and let out a shrill, high-pitched laugh.

He had black curly hair down past his shoulders and a short black beard. His green eyes rolled wildly in his head. He had an animal snout in place of a nose. He wore a dark fur waistcoat, very hairy, over black leather trousers, and furry brown slippers that came to a point.

"I'm free!" the dwarf-creature proclaimed, shouting at the top of his lungs. He waved his tiny hands high over his head. "I'm free as a bird! Thank you! Thank you all!"

"Hey, wait!" I cried.

But he scampered over the floor. Pulled open the kitchen door. And vanished into the rain.

Emily sank into her chair, her hands still

pressed against her cheeks. Kyle didn't move. He still had his hands balled into tight fists, ready for a fight.

I swallowed hard and waited for my heart to stop racing.

Kyle finally broke the silence. "A Krel. That guy was a Krel," he murmured, shaking his head.

I swallowed again. I stared out of the window. The rain had stopped. But I couldn't see anything out there.

"He looked just like the Krel in the pile of Character cards," Emily said.

"Huh?" I gazed down at the Be Afraid box. "Yeah. He did."

I grabbed the box and spilled the cards on to the kitchen table. I began shuffling frantically through the cards. "Where is that card? Where *is* it?"

I flipped through every card to the bottom of the pack. No Krel card.

"I went too fast. I know it's in here," I said.

I pushed the pack together and started going through it again, slower this time, carefully studying each card.

The king, a mutant dwarf, three Jekel cards, two Goths, a masked knight...

"Come on. Come on," I chanted, dropping each card on the table.

"It's gone," I announced, raising my eyes to my

two friends. "The Krel card has disappeared."

"Let me see those," Kyle snapped, scowling.

He grabbed for the pack and a card slid off the table and fell on the floor.

I bent quickly to pick it up.

A dragon card.

It showed an enormous dragon, wild-eyed, its head arched high, mouth open in a furious roar, flames shooting out of its nostrils.

I grabbed the card.

And heard slow, heavy, lumbering footsteps in the hall.

"The dragon!" I gasped.

I threw the card on to the table. Emily and Kyle stood frozen, eyes wide, mouths open.

"It's the dragon," I repeated, turning to the doorway.

"Connor? What dragon?" a familiar voice called.

Mum and Dad strode into the kitchen, drenched from the rain. Mum's curly brown hair was matted flat on her head. Raindrops slid down her cheeks. Dad's blue work shirt was soaked through.

"Uh . . . we were playing a game," I explained.

My hands were shaking. I grabbed the edge of the table so they couldn't see them.

"At least you didn't get caught in that sudden downpour," Mum said, kicking off her soaked trainers.

Dad stepped up to the table. "Did you see what happened next door? Didn't you hear the commotion?"

"What a disaster!" Mum added. "The poor Nelsons..."

"Huh? What happened?" I demanded.

Dad shook rainwater from his hair. "Go and take a look. It—it's incredible!"

"I can't believe you didn't hear it," Mum said, frowning.

I took off to the kitchen door, threw it open, and burst outside. Emily and Kyle followed close behind me.

The rain had stopped. The heavy, dark clouds were pulling apart, allowing shafts of late afternoon sunlight to filter through.

I ran past the wooden picket fence that separates our gardens. Then I slid to a stop on the wet grass as the Nelsons' house came into view.

I should say, what was *left* of their house!

The house had been trashed.

The windows were all broken. Shutters lay scattered over the wet ground. One wall was on its side, clumps of bricks everywhere. Half the roof had fallen into the house.

The hedge along the front drive had been trampled. The flowers in the garden at the side had all been uprooted. The mailbox lay on its side in the mud.

Neighbours circled the house in a hushed silence. I saw Mr and Mrs Nelson talking to two grim-faced police officers. They were both talking furiously at once, gesturing wildly with their hands.

"What happened?" I asked one of our neighbours. "Was it the storm?"

She shrugged. "I don't think so. The Nelsons say they were attacked."

I gasped.

I could hear Mr Nelson's voice as I stepped over broken glass and moved closer. "It was some kind of army!" he declared, shaking his head. "They were dressed up—like knights or something!"

Knights?

Mrs Nelson started to sob. "It was so frightening!" she cried. "They were on horseback. They—they wore metal helmets. We couldn't see their faces. They—they—" Her husband slid his arm round her, trying to comfort her.

"They attacked the house," Mr Nelson told the officers. "It was like a movie or something. I know it sounds crazy. But it's the truth. Knights on horseback, attacking our house."

I shrank back. My throat tightened. I couldn't swallow. My legs suddenly felt weak.

It wasn't a movie, I knew.

It was our game. Be Afraid.

In the game, I had sent my knights to attack the neighbouring castle.

And the Nelsons were attacked by an army of masked knights.

31

I suddenly felt sick. I covered my mouth. Waited for my stomach to settle down.

What can I do? I asked myself. How can I explain?

The police officers were arguing with the Nelsons. They didn't believe the wild story.

But I did.

I knew this was my fault. I knew the card game had caused this.

I looked up—and saw someone staring at me from the deep shadows behind the trampled hedge. He stepped over the hedge, out into the light.

Mr Zarwid.

His eyes locked on me, his expression set in a cold scowl.

I took a step back. Prepared to run to the safety of my house.

Mr Zarwid moved quickly, taking long strides across the wet grass. His yellow raincoat flew behind him. His big belly bounced up and down with each step.

"Anything you want to tell me, young man?" he rasped, staring hard into my eyes. "Anything you want to tell me about my missing pack of cards?"

He knows, I realized. Mr Zarwid knows that I stole his card game.

What does he plan to do? What is he going to do to me?

Mr Zarwid's tiny, round eyes burned into mine like lasers. Beneath the stiff white moustache, he muttered angrily to himself, his face set in a deep frown.

I swallowed hard. I can't tell him the truth, I decided. I can't tell him that I stole his card game.

I can't tell *anyone* that I'm responsible for the attack on the Nelsons' house.

Behind Mr Zarwid, the police officers were shaking their heads. Clustered in small groups, the neighbours were muttering in low voices, their expressions confused.

"I don't know anything," I told Mr Zarwid in a trembling voice. My thudding heart seemed to rise into my throat, choking me. I coughed. Took a deep breath. "I don't know anything about your pack of cards," I repeated.

Then I spun away and started to run over the slick, wet grass.

I had to get away. I had to think about this. I had to think hard, to decide what I should do.

I didn't wait for Emily and Kyle. I didn't turn back.

I kept running until I reached the safety of the house. Then I ran upstairs, slamming my bedroom door behind me.

Breathing hard, my entire body drenched in a cold sweat, I dropped down on to the edge of my bed. Head spinning, heart pounding.

I shut my eyes and saw the bold lettering on the card game box: BE AFRAID. BE VERY AFRAID.

That night, I dreamed about Mr Zarwid.

Dressed all in white, a white suit, white shirt, white tie—all as white as his hair and moustache—he rose up in front of me.

In the dream, he lifted his hands high above his head and boomed, *"Be afraid, Connor!"*

And then he turned to the door and waved his arms as if directing traffic.

I saw myself sit up in bed. I saw my startled expression.

I heard heavy footsteps outside my room. Grunts and cries and loud moans.

Mr Zarwid waved his arms harder. He threw back his head, his white hair falling to his shoulders, and let out a booming laugh.

A knight in shiny grey armour tromped into

my room. His broad shield banged against the side of the doorway.

"Hey—go away!" I cried out.

In the dream, I knew I was dreaming. But fear choked my throat and I uttered a shrill scream as other figures followed the clumping knight.

Goths and Krels. Bearded dwarf-creatures with animal snouts. Masked knights. Creatures with pigs' heads and human bodies.

Tossing back their heads, they howled and groaned and barked like animals.

So loud. So loud, I covered my ears.

But I couldn't drown out the sound of their groans and cries as they began to fight.

Slashing at each other with swords and long-bladed, gleaming daggers. Heaving themselves, banging armoured chest against armoured chest. Thrusting their shields in front of them, screaming and crying.

They tumbled over my bed. Slashed the window curtains. Sent everything on my desk clattering to the floor.

A battling Krel sent a masked knight toppling backwards into my bedroom window. The glass shattered and fell in a thousand pieces. A sword ripped through the wallpaper.

"Get out! Get out! Get out!" I shrieked. A desperate, terrified chant.

"Get out! Get out!" I woke up screaming. And

trembling. Drenched with sweat. My pyjama shirt stuck wetly to my back.

I sat up in bed, wide awake. Orange morning sunlight streamed through the curtains.

The window—not broken. Not broken.

The wallpaper not slashed.

I breathed a sigh of relief and started to climb to my feet.

But I dropped back down when I saw my floor. The carpet—stained with mud. Muddy footprints. Dozens of them, big and small.

Muddy footprints caked over the rug.

"No!" A terrified cry escaped my throat.

"It's the cards," I murmured out loud. I hugged myself, tried to force myself to stop shaking.

"It's the card game."

I had to get rid of the card game. I knew I wasn't safe while I still had it. I had to return it to Mr Zarwid.

I pulled myself to my feet.

I'll return them right now, I decided. I'll get dressed and run them over to Mr Zarwid's house.

Maybe I'll just leave the pack on his front doorstep.

Yes. That's it.

No need to talk to him. No need to hear his lecture about how stealing is wrong.

I know all that. I've learned my lesson.

I began to feel a little better, a little more steady. I had a plan. I knew what to do.

I pulled on a pair of jeans and a T-shirt. My hands trembled as I tied my laces.

I took a deep breath.

Connor, you're going to be okay, I told myself. You're going to return the cards, and your life will be totally normal again.

Where did I leave the cards? On my dresser.

Okay. Okay. No problem.

In a few minutes, everything will be fine again. I crossed the room to my dresser—and gasped.

The cards had gone.

Gone.

My hands fumbled over the clutter on the top of the dresser. No. No cards.

Frantically, I pulled open the drawers and searched. No cards.

I dropped to my knees and looked under the dresser. No cards.

I heard voices from downstairs. A girl's laugh. A chair scraped.

Oh. Wait. I must have left the cards downstairs. On the kitchen table.

Shaking my head, I climbed to my feet and hurried down to the kitchen.

"Hey!" I cried out in surprise. Emily and Kyle sat at the kitchen table. Kyle had separated the pack of cards into the four piles.

"We've been waiting for you," Emily said. "We didn't want to wake you."

"Grab some breakfast and let's play," Kyle urged. He shuffled one of the stacks of cards.

"No way!" I cried. "Put the cards back in the box, Kyle. I'm returning them to Mr Zarwid. Right away."

"Huh?" Kyle's mouth dropped open. "You can't do that. We're in the middle of a game."

"You've just defeated a castle," Emily chimed in. "You're winning. You have to give the Goth and the Krel a chance to catch you."

"No way!" I insisted again. "What's wrong with you two? The game is too dangerous. Didn't you see the house next door? Mr Zarwid warned us. He said—"

"He's a creepy old guy," Kyle sneered. "He hates kids. You know that."

"He was just trying to scare us," Emily said, shuffling a pile of cards. "You didn't fall for that warning—did you, Connor? It was so lame."

"But—but—" I sputtered. "The Nelsons' house?"

"It got wrecked in the storm," Kyle said.

"But it didn't start to storm until we drew a lightning card!" I exclaimed shrilly.

They both laughed. "Whoa. Do you really think you can control the weather now, Connor?" Kyle demanded.

"Sit down," Emily ordered. "You're wasting time. We could be playing."

I stared at them both. I could see they had their minds made up. They were going to keep playing no matter what I said.

39

"Okay, okay," I muttered.

I poured myself a glass of orange juice. Then I took my place at the table. "One more game," I insisted. "I mean it, guys. One more. That's all. Then I return the pack to Mr Zarwid."

Emily shuffled the cards in her hand. Then she set them face down on the table.

All three of us leaned forward as she started to draw a card.

I felt a chill at the back of my neck.

Should we have stopped? Were we making a horrible mistake?

Emily drew a card. Turned it over.

And I let out a cry.

Emily turned over a dragon card.

On the front of the card, the dragon rose up, deep silver, its long neck pulled back as if ready to attack. Long metallic spikes stood straight up angrily, stretching the length of its back. Its chest appeared plated, as if it were wearing armour. Broad silver wings poked up from its shoulders.

The dragon's long snout was open in a roar, revealing two rows of jagged teeth. The flaring nostrils shot out twin flames, red fire and smoke.

The three of us stared at the card. "Emily, pick a Fate card," Kyle instructed. He shoved another stack of cards towards her.

Emily hesitated for a moment. Then she pulled the card off the top of the Fate pile. She held it up. It showed two long black arrows curving round so that they pointed at each other.

"What does it mean?" Emily asked Kyle.

"It's a Switch card," he explained. "You switch

characters. You're not a Goth now. You switch to the dragon."

"Yessss! I'm the dragon now!" Emily declared happily.

I shut my eyes. And pictured my dream again. The howling, roaring figures, so ugly and strange, battling across my bedroom.

I don't like this, I thought. I don't want to be playing this game.

When I opened my eyes, Kyle was shoving the dice across the table to Emily. "Power up," he instructed. "Let's see how strong your dragon is." He sniggered. "You might just be a big, weak gasbag."

Emily sent the four dice rolling across the table. Two sixes, a five and a four.

"Wow! Awesome!" Kyle declared, pounding the table with his big fist. "Awesome! That dragon is *tough*!"

I had a heavy feeling in the pit of my stomach.

"I'm still king, right?" I asked Kyle. "And I still have my army of knights?"

He nodded.

"Well . . . I'm going to send my knights out to destroy the dragon," I announced.

I reached for the dice. Kyle pushed my hand away.

"First it's my turn," he said. He grinned at Emily. "The Krel has decided to team up with the dragon."

"Huh? What does *that* mean?" I demanded.

"Krels are very smart, very crafty," Kyle replied. "We know when to move to the other side."

"But what does that *mean*?" I repeated.

"I'm sharing my power with the dragon," he said.

"Yessss!" Emily cried. She reached across the table to slap Kyle a high five. "We rule!"

"But that's not fair!" I protested.

Kyle laughed. "This is war, Connor."

Kyle drew a card off the top of the pack and turned it face up. It showed a bearded elf in a brown apron holding a wide net.

"An elf fisherman," Kyle announced. He rolled the dice. Then he turned to me. "You're in trouble, King. The Krel has called together an army of two thousand elf fishermen. The elves sneaked past your army and threw their nets over you."

"You're kidding," I muttered.

He shook his head solemnly.

"You mean I've been captured?" I cried.

"Yes. Captured," Kyle announced. He shoved the dice to Emily. "The king is captured—and here comes the dragon to finish him off."

"No—wait!" I insisted.

But Emily rolled the dice.

And from out on the street, I heard a roar.

And then a woman screaming.

The squeal of car tyres. A loud *CRASH*.

And then another furious animal roar, louder and closer.

No—please, no! I silently prayed, watching the startled looks on my friends' faces.

Please don't let the dragon come to life. Please. . .

I jumped up and ran to the window.

I heard more shouts. Another car squealing to a stop.

But I couldn't see anything out the back.

I turned and ran to the front door. Emily and Kyle were close behind me. I pushed open the door—and heard another ferocious roar.

Not like any sound I'd ever heard before.

Not the hoarse, deep-throated roar of a lion or tiger. Not the bleating roar of an elephant.

This roar sounded like a low, rumbling boom of thunder that rose from deep inside an animal's belly. It grew louder and louder until it was a roar and a shrill shriek at the same time.

I heard a cracking sound, the sound of a tree falling.

More screams.

Emily, Kyle and I bolted down my front lawn. We stopped at the kerb as a broad shadow swept over the street.

And rising over its shadow, I saw the dragon.

Tall and spiked and furious—just like the portrait on the game card.

"I—I don't believe it!" I stammered.

The silvery wings rose up on its spiky back. The wings stretched—stretched like a ship's sail unfurling—and cut through power lines over the side of the street. Electricity crackled, and sparks flew as the lines came down.

Tilting its massive head up in another furious roar, the dragon's bulky body lumbered forward, sending the electrical poles tumbling to the ground.

The dragon raised a giant foot—and crushed a small blue car beneath it.

Neighbours were screaming and running. I heard kids crying. I saw a car squeal out of control and spin on to someone's front lawn.

Kyle stood beside me, staring open-mouthed at the giant, lumbering creature. "A dragon . . . a real dragon," he murmured.

"We brought it here," I said, grabbing his arm. "We set it loose. We have to do something about it."

He turned to me, his face twisted in fear. "Do something? Like *what*?"

"Well—"

"I have an idea," Emily interrupted breathlessly.

The dragon bellowed again as it crushed another car underfoot.

"Hurry—" Emily urged. "Into the house." She started to run across the lawn.

I took one last glimpse at the dragon as angry flames burst from its snout. Then I ran after Emily. "What's your idea?" I called.

She didn't answer until the three of us were back in the kitchen. "The card," she said, panting. "The dragon card. If we shove it back in the box, maybe the dragon will disappear."

"Yes!" I cried. "Remember last night? The storm stopped when we put the cards back in the box?"

"It might work," Kyle agreed.

We all jumped at the sound of a loud crash. Another tree falling? So close. Right outside the window.

We dived to the table and began frantically fumbling through the cards.

"Where is it?" I cried. "Where is the dragon?"

"I left it face up," Emily declared. "Remember? I had it right in front of me!"

Kyle slammed his fist on the table, sending a bunch of cards flying. "It isn't here!" he cried.

I didn't give up. I flipped through the cards again. But Kyle was right.

The dragon card had vanished.

"Now what?" Emily groaned.

I heard more screams from outside. Sirens

47

rising and falling. Another crash of splintering wood.

A chill shot down my back. I stared at a card on the table. And had an idea.

"The Masked Knight," I murmured out loud.

Emily and Kyle turned to stare at me. "So what?" Kyle snapped.

I grabbed for the dice. "I'm going to send a huge army of masked knights out to defeat the dragon," I announced.

"But—" Emily started.

I didn't let her finish. "It's worth a try," I said. "I just need to roll a *lot* of power points."

Kyle slapped me on the back for encouragement. "Good luck, Connor. Roll all sixes. Hurry!"

Another roar outside. The crackle of electricity. Shouts and terrified cries all down the street.

I squeezed the dice in my hand. Shook them. Shut my eyes and prayed for all sixes.

Then I lowered my hand and sent the dice tumbling on to the table.

"Oh, noooooo," I moaned.

Three ones and a two.

"Roll again," Emily urged. "Try again, Connor."

I started to reach for the dice again. But a clattering outside made me stop. I pushed myself away from the table and hurried to the front window.

"Oh, wow," I murmured. I saw five masked knights on the street. They moved together, marching slowly. They held their shields in front of them with one hand. Their swords were raised high in the other hand.

Their armour gleamed in the sun—until they stepped into the shadow of the dragon. And then all five of them seemed to fade into the deep grey of the shadow.

"Not much of an army," Kyle murmured. "If only you'd thrown all sixes, then maybe—"

He didn't finish his sentence.

All three of us gasped as the dragon lifted the first two knights in his giant jaws—and with a sharp toss of his head heaved them over the roof of the house across the street.

The ferocious creature lowered its head again. With a roar, it sent three angry bursts of orange flames over the remaining three knights.

Shrieking in horror, the knights dropped their swords and shields, turned and ran, their screams drowning out the clanking of their armour.

"The dragon wins," I muttered.

And then I watched, frozen in terror, as the dragon turned its massive body towards my house. It pulled back its head in an angry roar of attack.

Its shadow swept over the house as the creature lumbered on to the front lawn.

"It—it's coming here!" I choked out. "It's coming after us now!"

The shadow swept darkly over the house. I suddenly felt cold, deep cold, as if the dragon blocked out all the heat of the sun.

I turned and forced myself away from the window.

Shivering, I ran to the kitchen.

I could hear the dragon lumbering across my garden. Every footstep shook the house.

I heard a tree crack and fall. Heard the crackle of electricity as power lines were cut.

"It's coming round the side of the house!" Emily shrieked.

The cold, dark shadow washed over the back garden now, then over the kitchen window.

"It—it followed us back here!" Kyle cried.

I raised my eyes to the kitchen window and saw the massive, armour-like chest of the dragon. The creature bumped into the back of the house, shaking the whole house, sending cracks down the plaster kitchen walls.

It lowered its head to the window, snapping its powerful jaws—and peered in with red-rimmed eyes the size of basketballs.

Emily let out a terrified screech. She stumbled from the window, backing out of the room. She tripped over Kyle, who was also backing away.

I let out a choked cry as a last, desperate idea flashed into my mind.

I dived to the table and swept the cards into both hands. Swept them into a single pile, my whole body shuddering.

Holding the pack in one hand, I grabbed the box with my other hand.

Shove the cards into the box, Connor, I ordered myself.

Maybe . . . maybe if you shove all the cards back into the box, the dragon will disappear.

Like last night.

Last night, I remembered, we slid the pack of cards back into the box—and the storm stopped and all the lights came back on.

The kitchen window-pane shook as the dragon bumped it heavily with its snout. The red-rimmed eyes glared in at us. The giant nostrils flared.

The dragon arched its head back.

In a second, it's going to crash right through the window, I realized.

No time. No time.

I started to jam the cards into the box.

Dropped the box!

"Nooooo!" I uttered a horrified wail.

Fell to my knees. Grabbed the box in my shaking hand.

Struggled to slide the pack of cards in.

Pushed them. Pushed the cards into the box.

And snapped the lid shut.

Would it work?

I heard a loud *POP*, like the sound of a giant balloon bursting.

A blinding flash of white light made all three of us cry out in surprise.

Blinking, I turned to the window. Morning sunlight flooded into the kitchen.

Silence out there now.

We dived to the window and peered out.

I could see enormous, deep footprints rutting the garden.

But no dragon. No dragon. It had vanished.

"Connor—you're a genius!" Kyle declared. He slapped me hard on the back, so hard I nearly went flying through the window.

Emily started to laugh. Before we realized it, all three of us were laughing, hugging each other gleefully.

We were so happy the dragon had gone.

But as I glimpsed the box of cards on the

kitchen table, I stopped laughing. "We've got to return these to Mr Zarwid—now," I said.

"He told us the truth," Emily murmured, staring warily at the pack, as if it might explode at any second. "He tried to warn us how dangerous the game was. But we didn't listen."

Kyle brushed his thick blond hair back off his forehead. "If Zarwid knew the cards were so dangerous, why was he selling them at a garage sale?" he demanded.

"Good question," Emily replied softly, her eyes still on the pack. She turned to me. "Of course, he didn't expect someone to *steal* them."

I could feel my face growing hot. "Don't worry. I'll never steal anything again!" I declared. "And no more role-playing games. From now on, I'm sticking to Go Fish!"

"We're wasting time," Kyle said. "Let's return the cards."

"Will you come with me?" I asked. "Maybe if all three of us go, Mr Zarwid won't give me such a hard time."

They exchanged glances, then nodded. "Okay. Let's go," Emily said.

I reached for the box of cards. As I picked it up, the lid slid open—and a card fell out and fluttered to the floor.

I bent to pick it up.

And cried out in surprise when I saw the

figure on the front of the card. "Check this out!" I cried. "I didn't see this card before."

I stood up and held out the card so they could see it.

"It—it's Mr Zarwid!" Emily declared.

Yes. There he was, his white hair glowing, his stiff white moustache standing straight out, his round blue eyes staring out of the card at us.

"Look what it says on the back," I said. I turned the card over so they could see the word WIZARD.

"It's a Wizard card," Kyle said thoughtfully. "Whoa. Hold on. Zarwid . . . Wizard. . . Get it?"

Yes. I got it.

Zarwid is an anagram of Wizard. If you mix up the letters in Mr Zarwid's name, you get *wizard*.

Emily grabbed the card and raised it to her face, frowning at it as she studied it. "Do you think he's a real wizard?" she asked.

"Maybe," I replied.

She lowered the card and her expression turned to fear. "Then what do you think he'll do to us when he finds out we took the cards?"

I slid the Wizard card into my T-shirt pocket. Then I tucked the deck of Be Afraid cards into a back pocket of my jeans.

The three of us stepped out of the front door and started down the front lawn.

We stopped at the giant, fallen maple tree at the kerb. It had toppled over power lines. The torn wires buzzed and crackled, sending a shower of sparks over the pavement.

Across the street, I saw a red hunk of crushed metal. "That used to be a car," I murmured to my friends.

They gazed open-mouthed at the wreckage and destruction all down the block. Crushed cars. Toppled trees and power lines. Deep holes in the street. Broken hedges. Trampled flower-beds.

Three police cars blocked off the street, the red lights on their roofs flashing silently.

People huddled in small groups, crying,

chattering excitedly, pointing to the damaged houses and crushed cars, shaking their heads in bewilderment and shock.

"We did this," I muttered. "It's all our fault."

"I can't believe it," Emily replied in a trembling voice. "I can't believe that card game is so *evil*."

I saw a group of neighbours watching us. I wondered if they knew that we were the guilty ones. I was the one who stole the evil cards. We were the ones who made the knights and soldiers and dragon appear.

What would happen to my friends and me if people found out?

What would people do to us? Would they sue my parents? Would my parents have to pay for all the damage?

What would my parents do to me?

The questions sent a wave of cold panic over me. My legs suddenly felt weak. I tried to blink away my sudden dizziness.

We passed the police squad cars. I could hear their radios crackling. Dark-uniformed officers were walking up and down the street, checking out the deep footprints in the tarmac, scratching their heads, their expressions puzzled.

As we reached the corner, Mr Zarwid's house came into view. The front door was shut and the windows were all dark. The morning newspaper still lay in the driveway.

"Look—Zarwid's house is perfectly okay," Kyle said, pointing. "And his garden is too."

I touched the pack of cards in my back pocket. "I hope he's at home," I murmured. "I really want to get rid of these cards."

We crossed the street and made our way over the neatly trimmed lawn to his front door.

I peered into the window. But the reflection of the sun formed a gold curtain over it.

Taking a deep breath, I climbed the three low steps and pushed the doorbell. I could hear it chime inside the house.

"Mr Zarwid? Are you in?" I called, my voice choked and shrill. "Mr Zarwid?"

No reply.

No footsteps in the house. Not a sound.

I pushed the doorbell again. And waited. My hands were suddenly ice-cold. I could feel the blood pulsing at my temples.

Of course you're afraid, Connor, I told myself. He's a wizard. He has strange, magical powers. Maybe he's an evil wizard.

And I had stolen something that belongs to him.

"Hear anything?" Kyle called from the drive. He and Emily had hung back. Now they huddled close together, watching me.

I tried the bell again. Then I pounded the front door with my fist.

To my surprise, the door swung open.

"Hey!" I cried out.

I poked my head inside. The front of the house stood in darkness. I took a deep breath—and smelled a sharp, sweet aroma. Spicy.

"Mr Zarwid?" I called. My voice echoed hollowly in the darkness.

I took another deep breath, trying to slow my racing heart. Then I pushed the door open a little further and stepped into the front hall.

"Helllllo?" I called. "Anybody home?"

I jumped back when I heard the shrill peal of laughter from the front room.

I backed towards the door and bumped into Emily and Kyle, who had followed me inside.

"He—he's here," I stammered. "He's ... laughing!"

Another high, shrill laugh.

"That sounds like a baby," Emily whispered, clinging close to me. "Or an animal."

I heard loud whoops of laughter. Shrill chattering.

Keeping close together, we followed a beam of pale sunlight across the floor into the living room. As my eyes adjusted to the brighter light, I saw a room full of old-fashioned-looking furniture—stiff-backed, wooden chairs; a cluttered desk; a battered piano; heavy, dark drapes over the windows; a silver ball resting on a small table.

More laughter.

I turned—and saw where it came from.

A monkey. A little brown monkey, hopping up

and down excitedly in a brass cage, chattering non-stop.

"He's so cute!" Emily cooed, stepping up to the cage.

The monkey stopped its shrill chattering and tilted its head, staring out at her.

"Do you think it's a pet?" Kyle asked, eyeing it warily. "Or do you think it used to be a person, and Zarwid turned him into a monkey?"

"He has always been a monkey!" a high, scratchy voice called from behind us.

Recognizing Mr Zarwid's voice, I spun to the doorway.

He stood squinting at us with those cold, round eyes. His normally slicked-down white hair stood up in clumps round his head. I could see striped pyjamas beneath his silky maroon robe.

"Mr Zarwid—" I started.

"What are you doing here?" he demanded angrily. "What time is it? Why did you wake me up? Or did you think the house was empty?"

"N-no," I stammered. "We wanted to see you. We—"

"Well? You're seeing me!" he cried. "Do you normally break into people's houses to see them?"

"No. The door swung open," I replied.

"We didn't break in," Kyle added, trying to help me. "We rang the bell several times."

"It's true," Emily added.

Mr Zarwid rubbed his chin. Then he straightened his moustache, still scowling at us. "I think I know why you came," he said finally.

"Uh . . . yeah," I choked out. I reached into my back pocket and pulled out the box of cards. "Here," I said, holding them out to him in a trembling hand.

His blue eyes flashed. "So you *did* steal them!" he declared.

"Yes. I took them," I murmured, lowering my eyes to the floor. "I—I'm sorry."

"And you played the game," he continued, crossing the cluttered room towards me. "And you called up a dragon. And you nearly destroyed your entire block!"

"I suppose so," I replied in a whisper. "We didn't mean to."

The cold eyes froze on me. "You didn't mean to play the game? You didn't mean to steal my cards?" he demanded, hovering over me.

"We didn't mean to wreck all the houses and cars," I choked out.

"We're really sorry," Kyle added.

"Yes. We're truly sorry," Emily chimed in.

"*Sorry isn't enough!*" Mr Zarwid boomed.

He grabbed the box of cards from my hand.

"Apologizing isn't enough," he said.

"What else can we do?" I cried. "I'm not a thief. I've never stolen anything before. I didn't know the cards were so—so powerful! It was all just a big mistake!"

"Yes," the old wizard agreed, fingering his moustache again, his eyes still locked on mine. "Yes, it was a big mistake. And now—now you know too much."

I took a step away from him and bumped into a high-backed sofa. "Know too much? What do you mean?" I demanded shrilly.

Emily and Kyle moved up beside me.

Mr Zarwid didn't answer the question. Instead, a strange smile played over his pale face. Keeping his eyes on us, he pulled the cards from the box.

"Since you like the cards so much," he said, his smile spreading, the thick moustache appearing to fly up like wings, "why not *live* the game?"

"Huh?" I gasped.

But before I could ask what he meant, he swept his arm up and threw the cards high in the air.

Threw them over Emily, Kyle and me.

They fluttered down, down, over us, over our heads, our shoulders. Fluttered silently down.

And as the cards fell, darkness came down with them.

A deep, cold darkness I had never seen or felt before.

The room faded behind it. Mr Zarwid vanished. Emily and Kyle disappeared.

I didn't move. But I felt myself falling. Falling into the dark, into the frigid cold.

Into stillness.

And then an explosion of pain made me scream.

Pain that shot out from my chest, through my arms, my legs. A burst of pain that made my head ring.

My head . . . my head. . .

I knew it was about to explode from the pain.

My eyes popped out. My teeth flew out of my mouth.

My brain shot out through my open, screaming mouth.

I know this cold darkness, I thought.

I know this chilling stillness.

It's death.

The cold seemed to wash away before the darkness did. I felt a wave of warmth. I blinked. Opened my eyes.

Stared into charcoal-black. Tiny pinprick lights shimmered in the black.

Stars?

Yes. I stared up at a starry, cloudless sky. The wind stirred. It fluttered my hair.

I'm on my knees, I realized. On my hands and knees in tall, damp grass.

The air smelled so fresh, so sweet.

I'm alive!

I heard a groan. The grass rustled beside me.

Emily crawled into view. She narrowed her eyes at me as if she didn't recognize me. She shook straw from her hair. "Connor, where are we?" she whispered.

"Yeah. Where are we?" Kyle followed her out of the tall grass.

"We're okay," I choked out, still feeling shaky.

"I thought my brain was exploding. I thought I'd died."

"But where *are* we?" Emily demanded. "It was morning—and now it's night."

I pulled myself up from my knees and gazed around. "We're in a wide field," I reported. "Very flat."

Emily and Kyle stood up too. "It's like a farm or something," Kyle murmured.

Beyond the flat field of tall grass, I saw small circles of orange flame. Tiny fires burning outside low, round huts.

"I think it's some kind of farm village," I said. "Check out the little houses. I think they're made of grass or straw."

"Weird," Kyle muttered, frowning.

Squinting into the grey night, I saw a tall mound of hay. A wooden wagon tilted down beside it. I saw other small, two-wheeled wagons. I heard a horse whinny somewhere in the distance beyond the rows of little huts.

Emily swatted at a fat purple insect on her neck. "I—I don't like it here," she stammered. She climbed to her feet. "I want to go home."

"I think we're a long way from home." I sighed. "What did Mr Zarwid say? I was so terrified, I could barely hear him."

"He said, 'Why not live the game?'" Kyle reported. "Then he threw the cards over us. And here we are."

"You mean we're *in* the game?" Emily cried. "We're in some land with masked knights and fire-breathing dragons?"

"That's impossible," I muttered.

"Yeah, sure. It's impossible," Kyle echoed, rolling his eyes. "It's impossible—but here we are."

"But—but—" I sputtered.

I dropped back to my knees when I heard a rasping cry.

I heard scraping footsteps. Saw the tall grass bend.

A long line of little men came into view, marching quickly across the field. They were dressed in ragged furs. The domelike metal helmets on their hairy heads glowed dully in the starlight. They carried long, pointed spears at their sides.

"*Hup hup hup hup*," they chanted as they marched.

"Jekels!" Kyle whispered, his eyes bulging wide with alarm.

All three of us ducked low behind the grass.

"I recognize them from the cards," he whispered. "They're evil. They're—"

"I read the back of the card," Emily whispered, shuddering. "They're evil hunters, right? And they're cannibals. They eat humans."

18

"Hup hup hup hup."

I stared in horror as they came marching towards us, spears up, spears down, raising them in a steady rhythm as they marched.

I took a deep breath and, ducking low behind the tall grass, started to move away.

"Hup hup hup hup."

Had they seen us? I wasn't sure.

I didn't wait to find out.

I half ran, half dived through the grass. Emily and Kyle were at my side.

We made our way silently over the soft ground, trying not to rustle the tall grass, listening for any sign that the evil little men had spotted us.

Where to go? Where to hide? My heart pounded against my chest. My breath burst out in panting gasps.

The tall mound of hay, shimmering dully under the pale starlight, rose up in front of us like a giant creature.

I didn't hesitate. I didn't think about it.

Lowering my head, I dived into the side of the haystack.

Damp and scratchy.

I covered my eyes with one hand and pushed deeper into the hay. It scratched my face. Prickled through my clothes. I felt sharp straws slide down the back of my neck.

A scuttling sound made me stop. I felt a sharp stab of panic in my chest.

Then I realized I was hearing Emily and Kyle burrowing into the hay beside me.

"Ooh, it's so *wet*!" Emily whispered.

"Did they see us?" Kyle asked.

"I—I don't know," I stammered, pulling a tuft of hay off my cheek. "Ssshh. Don't talk. Just listen."

Silence now, except for the scratching, scuttling of the hay around us.

I couldn't hear the thuds of the Jekels' marching feet. And I didn't hear their *"hup hup hup"* marching chant.

Had they gone?

Or were they waiting for us to come out?

Hay prickled my face. I pulled a damp strand out of my nose.

"I'm so itchy," Emily whispered.

And as she said it, I started to itch too. My back . . . my chest . . . my cheeks. . .

My skin tingled and burned.

70

Tingled. . .

I twisted and squirmed, trying to move the hay. I couldn't scratch. I couldn't try to rub the painful itching away.

I gritted my teeth. So itchy . . . so itchy. . .

"Ohh. . ." I uttered a low moan when I realized why.

Fat purple insects. I pulled one off my face. I scraped another one off the back of my hand.

I felt them on the back of my neck. Sliding down my T-shirt. Slithering over my back.

Hundreds of them, fat purple insects crawling through the hay. Crawling over us. . .

"Yucccck." I started to gag as an insect prickled across my cheek and tried to slide into my mouth.

I spat it out. It left a sour taste on my lips. I gritted my teeth. Forced myself not to gag again.

I spat once more. Scratched my face. Scratched my chest. Tried to rub my tingling back against the hay.

But it didn't help.

I'm going to itch to death! I thought.

I felt like screaming. Like bolting out from under the insect-infested hay, screaming my lungs out. I wanted to tear off my clothes. Tear off my skin!

I'll never stop itching, I told myself. I'm going to itch like this for the rest of my life!

"I—I can't take this much longer," I heard

Emily whisper from somewhere close beside me. "I've got to get out of this hay. I've got to scratch!"

"Ssshhh," Kyle warned. "I think the Jekels are still out there."

I couldn't stop shivering. The straw pressed against me, so wet and scratchy.

I pulled a fat insect out of my ear.

And then I felt one crawl up my nose.

No! I ordered myself. Connor—don't sneeze. Don't sneeze. . .

"AH-CHOOOOOOOO!"

Before my sneeze ended, I heard gruff shouts. Angry grunts.

No time to move. I heard a rush of footsteps.

And then hands grabbed me roughly, wrapped round my arms, my neck—and several Jekels pulled me out from the hay.

Chattering rapidly in a language I didn't recognize, the little men pulled Emily and Kyle out and shoved them hard into the open area at the side of the haystack.

They surrounded us quickly, at least a dozen of them, jabbing the points of their spears at us, chattering away, their expressions hard and angry.

I scratched my chest. Pulled an insect out from under my shirt and threw it to the ground. My two friends were also scratching furiously, pulling off insects.

I could see the fat insects crawling in Emily's

hair. I reached over and pulled four or five of them out for her.

Finally, I took a deep breath and turned to our captors. "Do you speak English?" I cried out in a high, shrill voice.

Their chattering stopped. Beneath their tangled, matted hair, the Jekels narrowed their eyes at us. They kept their spears poised.

"English?" I repeated. "Anyone?"

They stared at us curiously, as if they didn't believe we could speak.

"Let us go!" Emily cried. "We don't belong here!"

Silence.

They edged the tips of the spears closer. The circle of Jekels closed in.

Emily, Kyle and I were forced to huddle close together.

I raised my eyes past the circle of little men, searching for a way to escape. Beyond them, I could see only flat fields, rows of little huts, a small fire burning outside each hut.

I swallowed hard. Nowhere to hide. No way to escape.

"Ow!" I cried out when I felt the jab of a spear in my back.

I jumped forward.

The Jekels grunted menacingly. They poked us from behind, jabbing hard, forcing us to move.

"Whoa! Wait!" I cried, unable to keep the panic from my voice. "Where are you taking us?"

More grunts and angry growls. I leaped forward as another spear point poked my back.

"If only we had an Invisibility spell," Kyle whispered as we were forced across the tall, wet grass. "Or maybe a Cloak of Invincibility."

"This isn't a game!" I choked out. "This is real!"

The Jekels forced us across the field. Shoved us up to a small, bright fire outside a low hut. Red embers crackled at the bottom of the fire, sparkling like jewels. The wood hissed as the flames reached out towards us, pushed by a strong breeze.

"What are they going to do—*cook* us?" Emily gasped.

"I—I don't know," I stammered.

"Jekels always kill their food before they eat it," Kyle whispered.

That didn't make me feel any better at all. A shudder ran down my body. My legs suddenly felt like rubber.

The Jekels formed a tight line in front of us, spears raised, keeping our backs close to the fire.

"We come in peace!" I cried. "We mean you no harm!"

"Let us go!" Emily wailed. "We don't live here! You have no right to keep us!"

They grunted among themselves, ignoring us. A few of them waved their spears, pushing us even closer to the darting flames.

"They're little. We can probably push right through them," I whispered to Kyle.

He shook his head. "Bad idea. Jekels are small. But they have inhuman strength."

I sighed. "What are we going to do?"

Kyle didn't have a chance to answer. We heard a scraping sound. A cough. And a Jekel dressed in white fur burst out through the low doorway of the hut.

The other Jekels instantly grew silent. They raised their swords at attention. They all stared solemnly at the man from the hut.

I studied him as he made his way over to us. The white fur of his waistcoat and trousers glowed in the firelight. He wasn't dark-haired like all the others. He had wavy blond hair down his back and gleaming blue eyes under a broad forehead.

"Visitors," he said, in a surprisingly deep voice. "Visitors," he repeated, as if trying out the word for the first time.

"You—you speak English?" I stammered.

He nodded, turning his intense gaze on me. "You do not look like knights," he said thoughtfully. "And you do not look like Krels."

Two Jekels stepped aside so that their leader could move close to us. "Are you Goths?" he demanded. "Are you sorcerers?"

The glow of the firelight flickered in his eyes. He pressed his hands against his waist and waited for an answer.

"We—we're just kids," I sputtered.

He narrowed his eyes. "Kids? Kids? Are you powerful?"

"No!" Emily cried. "We have no power at all. Let us go—please!"

"We didn't come to fight," I told him. "We are not fighters. We are ... students. We're just kids."

He rubbed his smooth chin. "Then why are you *kids* here?"

"We—we don't know," Kyle replied. "We were sent here by a wizard. We don't—"

The Jekels all cried out. They raised their spears.

Their leader's eyes grew wide. "By a wizard? So you *are* sorcerers?"

"No!" I screamed. "We have no powers. It's all a mistake. A horrible mistake!"

He studied us one by one. "We'll see," he muttered finally.

He barked a command to his men. Two of the Jekels ran to the next hut and disappeared inside.

A few seconds later, they reappeared. One of

them carried a large silver goblet in front of him. He held it carefully in both hands.

The leader took the goblet from him and lowered it so that we could see inside. I saw a dark liquid in the silver cup, churning, bubbling, about to boil over.

"Ohh." I pulled my head back in disgust. It smelled like rotting meat.

"You will drink this," the Jekels' leader declared, raising the goblet towards me.

"No way!" I choked out.

My stomach lurched. I clamped a hand tightly over my mouth.

I couldn't get the sickening aroma out of my nostrils. It was the worst thing I'd ever smelled, like decaying meat and rotten fish and skunk odour, all in one.

The thick black liquid dribbled over the side of the goblet.

"Drink it quickly," the Jekel ordered. "It won't taste as bad if you drink it down fast."

"But—what *is* it?" I uttered in a choked whisper.

"Poison," he replied. "A deadly poison."

I gasped. "But—why?"

"It is our Truth Test," he declared. "If you drink it and survive, it means you are telling the truth."

I stared at the bubbling black liquid. "But—has anyone ever survived?" I cried.

He shook his head. "No. Not yet."

I gagged. The foul stench from the steaming cup was choking me, sickening me.

"Drink," he ordered. "You must take our Truth Test. Drink it down—now."

He held my head with one hand. And with his other hand, pushed the goblet to my lips.

I felt the hot, tarlike liquid against my mouth.

The sour stench steamed over my face.

A deafening roar made my ears throb.

The goblet fell from the Jekel's hand. The thick liquid spread over the dirt.

Another roar. The ground began to tremble.

The Jekel leader staggered back, his eyes wide with surprise.

I licked my lips. I could taste the poison.

My stomach heaved.

But I forgot all about it as an enormous dragon lurched into view.

Another roar.

Another dragon appeared, lumbering over the grassy field. And then another.

And I saw figures riding high on the dragons' arched necks. Armoured figures riding the sharp spikes on the backs of the lumbering creatures.

Knights with swords and shields, glowing in the light from the fires.

The dragons shrieked furiously, snapping their toothy jaws, treading over the haystack, flattening it under their broad feet. A dragon stormed over the leader's hut, crushing it underfoot like a paper cup.

The helmeted, armoured knights hung from the dragons' long necks, lowering themselves, holding on with one hand as they swung their swords in wide circles at the startled Jekels.

The field rang out with cries. The triumphant battle cries of the knights. The high, shrill shrieks of the advancing dragons. The terrified moans and whimpers of the Jekels.

The evil little men dropped their spears and ran. The leader ran after them, calling for them to stay and fight.

Kyle shoved me hard. "Wow! It's just like in the game!" he uttered, eyes wide with amazement.

"Let's go!" Emily cried.

And we took off, running away from the Jekels, away from the shouting, swooping knights on their dragons, away from the huts and fires.

Our feet thudded over the soft ground. We were running at full speed, running over a wide dirt field. Escaping from the battle. Escaping from the evil Jekels.

Breathing hard, my chest throbbing, I turned back.

The huts were all burning now, bright flames

flying up against the purple night sky. The whole grassy field appeared to be on fire.

The Jekels had all vanished. The knights on their dragons were whooping and cheering and swinging their swords high above their heads in triumph.

"Keep going," Kyle urged, pulling my sleeve as we ran. "Don't stop. Those knights may be our enemy too."

"If they come after us..." Emily gasped. "We're dead meat."

I glanced back again. In the light of the burning huts, I saw them still celebrating their victory.

"It wasn't a very fair fight," I said, taking a long, deep breath of cool air.

"Who cares?" Kyle cried. "You almost had to drink that poison!"

"Ohhh." The thought of it sickened me all over again.

I turned and started to run faster.

The flat field curved down, then tilted uphill again. A line of tall stalks rose up like a wall in front of us.

"We can hide in the corn stalks!" I cried.

We lowered our heads and dived into the tall, dry stalks, shoving them aside, pushing them with our shoulders, our shoes crunching over dried leaves at our feet.

The stalks rose up high over our heads. They

crackled and creaked, bending away as we moved through them.

After a minute or so, I stopped. Panting hard, I lowered my hands to my knees and struggled to catch my breath.

All round us, the tall stalks rustled and swayed.

"We're safe here," Emily said softly. "At least for a while."

"Yeah. No one can see us in here," Kyle agreed.

"I've never seen corn stalks this tall," I said, still breathing hard. "They're so thick and—"

I stopped with a choked gasp when I saw a stalk in front of me begin to open.

I saw a quick movement.

A hand. A slender hand reaching out from inside the stalk.

Stalks crackled around us. Creaked and swayed.

And opened.

Hands slid out first. And then slender, dark bodies, smooth and shiny, moved out from the unfurling stalks.

Dozens of slender, silent creatures. With smooth green heads. No features. No faces. Leafy green heads like ears of corn before they've been shelled.

Dozens—and then hundreds of them.

The stalks creaked open, swaying softly, as the creatures moved out.

The slender, dark arms stretched, stretched out from the stalks like rubber. The hands slid round us. Tightening. . .

Tightening. . .

"Stelks!" Emily choked out. "Remember the card, Connor? They're Stelks!"

"I—I don't remember," I gasped.

Hands wrapped round my chest, my throat. And tightened. Tightened like vines.

"Can't breathe. . ." I heard Kyle groan. "Can't breathe. . ."

I squirmed and kicked.

But the creatures held on tightly.

Too many of them. Too many to fight.

And still the stalks opened, unfurled, letting loose more silent, deadly Stelks.

"What can we do?" I choked out. "What can we do now?"

YOU FINISH THE STORY.

I slammed the book shut.

"What a cheat!" I cried angrily. "What a stupid, stupid cheat!"

My sister, Amy, glanced up from her magazine. "What's your problem, Mark?" she demanded. "You've been reading that book for hours. I thought you liked it."

"I *did* like it!" I declared, shoving the book away. "But it's a total cheat."

Amy shook her head. Her curly blonde hair bounced like a sponge.

I have curly hair too. But it's dark and the curls aren't so tight and tiny. And I don't have a round head and look like a baby doll!

Amy is eleven, just one year younger than me. But she always acts as if she's my older sister or something.

"You like all those books with knights and dragons," she muttered. "Bor-rring."

"It wasn't boring. It was exciting," I insisted.

"These kids were playing a card game and—"

"Oooh. Thrills and chills!" Amy exclaimed, rolling her big blue doll's eyes.

Do I need a sister who is totally sarcastic all the time?

Yeah. Like I need a hairy wart on my nose!

"But then the book gets to a really exciting part," I continued. "And—and when it gets totally intense, it just says: *you finish the story*."

"Wow. That *is* a total cheat," Amy agreed. She closed her magazine and dropped down on the floor beside me. She reached for the book. "What's it called, Mark?"

"It's called *Be Afraid*," I told her. "It's about a kid named Connor."

"Connor?"

"Yeah. Connor Buckley. He steals a pack of cards. But it turns out to be a really evil card game with dragons and knights and stuff."

"Cool," Amy said.

"Yeah," I agreed. "It turns out that the guy Connor stole the card game from is a wizard. And when Connor tries to return the cards, the wizard is really angry. So he sends Connor and his two friends *into* the game."

Amy stared at me. "So they have to fight the dragons?"

"Well, yeah," I replied. "But then they get caught by these weird stalk creatures. And before they can defeat them or escape, the book just ends. And it says, *You finish the story*."

Amy laughed. She has a high, squeaky giggle that makes my teeth itch.

"I suppose the author ran out of ideas," she said.

"I suppose so," I replied unhappily.

Amy picked up the book and flipped through the pages. "Oh, wow!" she exclaimed. "I've found something. Look. Something tucked in a pocket in the back cover."

She slid her hand into the back cover and pulled out something.

A pack of cards.

She handed them to me.

I turned them over and flipped through them. Krels . . . dragons . . . Jekels. . .

"It's the card game!" I cried excitedly. "It's the cards from the book! Wow!"

"Cool," Amy replied.

Her favourite word. For a few weeks, she tried saying "brilliant" all the time. Everything was "brilliant". But then she went back to "cool".

I shuffled through the cards. I started to separate the Power cards from the Character cards. "Go and get some dice," I told Amy. "Let's try it."

She tilted her head and squinted at me. Her spongy hair bounced on her head. "You mean try the game?"

"Sure," I replied, separating out the Fate

cards. "It'll be fun. We don't have anything else to do—right?"

It was nearly the end of summer, and Amy and I were both pretty bored.

Mum and Dad had travelled to France for two weeks, but they'd left us behind. Our cranky grandmother was staying with us.

Early in the summer, I had a job stocking shelves in my uncle's shoe shop for a few weeks. But it was too boring. I begged Mum and Dad to let me leave, and they finally did.

So Amy and I just hung out for the rest of the summer. It was bor-rring—not brilliant!

"I don't know if I want to play," Amy said. "Those cards look really creepy."

"It'll be fun," I insisted. "The game is only a little creepy. It's exciting once you get into it."

She hesitated. "But you said it was dangerous."

"It's just a card game," I said. "It's like storytelling. You make up the story as you go along."

"Well . . . okay. But just for a few minutes." Amy came back a short while later with four dice. She dropped down opposite me on the floor. "I want to go first," she insisted.

Typical.

"Okay," I said. I pointed to a pile of cards face down on the floor. "You have to pick a character first. This is the character you will play for the whole game. Go ahead. Pick a card."

She spread the cards out and studied the backs. And studied them. And studied them.

"Amy—there's nothing to see!" I cried. "You're staring at the backs!"

"Okay, okay," she moaned.

She picked a card.

Turned it over.

And the room went black.

We both uttered startled cries.

"Hey—who turned out the lights?"

"What's happening?"

Suddenly, I couldn't breathe. I felt a heavy weight, as if someone was standing on my chest.

I dropped on to my back, gasping, choking, desperately trying to suck in air.

And then my arms and legs shot out. My chest felt about ready to burst. My skin pulled tight against my body.

I'm being *pulled apart*! I thought.

"Ohhhh." A long, low moan escaped my throat.

I realized I could breathe again. I took several deep, noisy breaths. The air felt cool and damp.

"Amy? Where are you? Are you okay?" I whispered.

Pale light filtered through the darkness. I gazed up at a white full moon, low in the sky.

I turned and saw Amy, sitting on the ground,

shaking her head, her hair bobbing, a dazed expression on her face.

She gazed up at the moon and then turned to me. "Mark—we're outside," she murmured. "We're not at home any more."

I climbed shakily to my feet and looked around. A cool breeze fluttered my T-shirt. I saw a long, flat, grassy field, stretching darkly under the pale moonlight. In the distance, I could see a tall haystack. And beyond it, tiny huts with a fire burning outside each hut.

"Where are we?" Amy demanded shrilly. She jumped up, dusted off the back of her shorts, then grabbed my arm. "Where are we? How did this happen? Where is our house?"

I swallowed hard. I couldn't answer any of those questions.

We both gasped when we heard the heavy, lumbering footsteps.

The ground shook with each step. It sounded like steady, booming thunder, low against the ground.

"Come on!" I cried, grabbing my sister's hand. Running hard over the muddy field, I pulled her behind a clump of tall grass.

BOOM...BOOM...BOOM...

The dragon stepped into the wide beam of moonlight. It rumbled over the field, its belly rising and falling, slender wings raised above its massive spiked shoulders.

"A—a dragon!" I gasped. "Just like in the story!"

With its long, plated neck arched high, the creature kept its gaze straight ahead. Jaws shut tightly, the huge head bobbed in rhythm to the heavy footsteps.

Amy squeezed my hand. We stared openmouthed at the creature as it lumbered past the clump of grass.

Will it see us? I wondered.

Can it smell us?

Is it *searching* for us?

No. It clomped steadly, heaving its body forward, big feet sinking into the mud, leaving a trail of deep holes behind it.

From the safety of our hiding-place, we watched it move until it stepped out of the moonlight, over the dark horizon, and disappeared.

I waited for my heart to stop racing. Then I whispered to Amy, "I know where we are."

She was still squeezing my hand. She let go and took an awkward step back, nearly tumbling into a tall bush. "Get us out of here," she choked out. "I don't *care* where we are. I just don't want to be here!"

"We're in the card game," I continued. I tried to sound calm, but my voice cracked.

Amy narrowed her eyes at me. "Get serious."

"I *am* serious," I insisted. "This is just what

happened to Connor and his friends in the book."

"That was a book," Amy wailed. "This is real life! I'm scared, Mark. We have to get home. I'm really scared!"

"I'm scared too," I confessed. I pictured that dragon tromping past us, so close. So close.

What if it had spotted us?

That thought sent a chill creeping down my back.

"What can we do?" Amy demanded shrilly. "How do we get back to our house? Do we say some magic words or something?"

"Magic words?" I stared at her, thinking hard. "No. No magic words. . ."

"Then *what*?" she screamed. "Do something! Do something! This was all your idea! I didn't want to play the stupid game!"

I grabbed her by the shoulders. "Amy—stop! Calm down," I pleaded. "Don't totally lose it. I'll think of something. But if you panic—"

"It's too late to panic!" she screamed. "I'm way past panic. I—I'm—"

"I have an idea," I told her, still gripping her shoulders. "Stop screaming and listen to me. I have an idea."

Her whole body trembled. Her eyes locked on mine, challenging me. "What? What idea?"

"The cards," I said, thinking hard, remembering what Connor had done. "When the kids in the book shoved the cards back into the box, everything returned to normal."

"Really?"

I nodded. "We just have to find the cards and the box."

I led the way out from behind the tall grass. We followed our footprints in the mud back to where they ended. We had to jump over the huge, deep, round footprint where the dragon had crossed our footprints.

"Here," I announced, pointing. "This is where we must have landed."

The muddy field shimmered under the white moonlight. The breeze picked up, the air was cool and damp.

"I can't see any cards," Amy said in a tiny voice.

We both bent low and searched the ground. We made wider and wider circles.

No cards.

I sighed. "The cards must still be on the floor at home. They didn't come here with us."

"Then how do we get back?" Amy demanded, her voice breaking. Her eyes watered over. I could see she was about to start crying.

"Let's start walking," she suggested. "Let's find a town. There's got to be a phone somewhere."

I took her shoulders again and turned her round. "You don't understand," I said softly.

"There are no phones. And probably no towns. We're in some kind of medieval world. With dragons and knights and elves and things."

Her mouth dropped open. A tiny squeak escaped her throat. I could see the panic in her eyes.

"Amy, we'll get out," I promised. "We'll find a way. It's only a game. It's just a card game."

"Well, we'll never find a way home if we just stand here in this field," Amy complained.

"You're right," I agreed. The cool wind made me shiver. "We're not safe out here, either." I pictured the clumping dragon again.

Maybe there were more dragons who crossed this field at night.

I turned and gazed at the thick forest of trees behind the clump of evergreens. "We'll be safer in the forest," I said. "Maybe we can find a path that leads somewhere."

Amy nodded but didn't say anything.

We started walking. I led the way into the trees, our shoes sinking into the soft forest ground.

We had walked only a few minutes when I stepped on something on the ground—a log or a tree branch.

I heard a sharp snapping sound.

And a heavy net dropped from the trees, fell over us, covered us.

"A trap!" I cried. "We've been captured!"

The heavy net forced us to our knees.

I struggled to shove it away. To lift it high enough to stand.

But the thick rope was rough and cut my hands. And I couldn't budge it.

"We've got to get out!" Amy wailed. "We've got to keep trying."

But we both quickly discovered that the net couldn't be moved.

Frightening questions flashed through my mind, too frightening to share with my sister.

What if this trap was set many years ago? What if no one checks the trap any more?

If no one comes, we'll starve to death under here, I realized.

But what if it was set recently? Who set it? I wondered. What were they trying to catch? Humans?

I shuddered as I remembered the Jekels in the story.

Amy and I both froze as we heard the crackle and scrape of shoes over the thick carpet of dead leaves on the forest floor.

"Someone's coming!" I whispered, my heart pounding.

"I hope he's friendly," Amy whispered back.

A short, stocky figure stomped up to the net. I gasped as he came into clear view.

He wore a shaggy suit of furs. He stood on two legs like a human. But his ears were pointed and poked up through his tuft of black hair like a pig's ears. He had a man's eyes but a pig-shaped snout and long walrus tusks descending from his lipless mouth.

"Hello!" Amy called out in a tiny voice. "Can you get us out of here?"

He stared into the trap, scratching his tuft of hair with long, three-fingered hands that ended in short claws.

"Hello? Do you speak English?" Amy tried again.

The creature grunted in reply, a harsh, raspy sound from deep in his stocky chest.

"Please—" I started.

But a high, sharp *YIP YIP YIP* made me stop.

A small, four-legged animal came bursting up beside the big creature. It yipped excitedly at us and pawed at the net with slender black hooves.

It was shaped like a dog, small like a dachshund, but instead of fur, it had smooth yellow skin. As it yipped, it opened its mouth to reveal two rows of tiny, sharp, pointed teeth.

The bigger man-creature grunted at the little creature and petted its head. The little dog-creature stopped yipping and purred like a cat.

The man grabbed the net and began to tug.

"He—he's letting us out!" I cried.

But I was wrong.

He kept Amy and me tightly wrapped up inside the net and began to tug us through the forest.

We couldn't slip free. The man had incredible strength. When we dropped to our backs and tried to roll out from under, he tugged harder and dragged us across the forest floor.

The little pet yipped and yapped, running ahead, then behind, circling us excitedly.

The man grunted as he tugged. Shiny gobs of wet drool ran down his walrus tusks, and he kept licking them off with a long blue tongue.

Amy and I bumped and stumbled and staggered and slid under the weight of the net. Finally, the man stopped tugging and let go.

With loud sighs, we dropped to our knees and squinted out through the net.

Where had he dragged us?

I saw a long, low, grey stone building. It had a narrow door at one end. No windows.

His house?

Grunting loudly, licking his tusks, the man stepped up to a smaller stone structure at the near side of the house. He pulled down a wide door in the front.

Flames shot out of the opening, leaping towards the sky.

The man took a shovel. Poked it into the fire. Stirred rapidly. Then I watched him throw in more coals.

"Mark—what *is* that?" Amy whispered.

I swallowed hard. "I think it's an oven," I replied.

Amy gasped. "You mean . . . he's going to *cook* us?"

I didn't reply. I stared out at the man. He was licking his tusks hungrily, stirring the oven coals, making the flames leap and dance.

"What are we going to do, Mark?" Amy cried. "You read the book. Do you have an idea? Any idea at all?"

I swallowed again. "No," I confessed. "No, I don't."

The man raked the coals once again, sending glowing red embers shooting out from the blazing oven. Then he threw his shovel aside and came lumbering towards us.

Beneath the walrus tusks, I saw a hungry grin spread over his piglike face. The yellow dog-creature panted excitedly, running in circles around the man as he approached us.

My temples throbbed. My heart thudded painfully in my chest. Desperate thoughts whirred through my mind.

"He has to lift the net now," I whispered to Amy. "As soon as he lifts it—run. He can't grab us both."

I was wrong.

Without removing the net, he shoved us up to the open oven. So close, the heat burned my face and I had to shut my eyes from the bright glare of the flames.

The net slid off.

And before Amy and I could move, the grunting man grabbed us by the front of our shirts, one in each hand.

He was so small—at least fifteen centimetres shorter than me—but his grip was so powerful, we could not struggle free.

"Noooooo—please!" I wailed. "Noooooo!"

He tugged us closer to the oven door.

"Stop!" Amy shrieked. "You can't! You CAN'T!"

He grunted in reply. His face showed no emotion at all.

Flames jumped from the open oven door. The heat burned my skin.

Still holding us each with one hand, he began to lift us off the ground—towards the oven door.

The dog-creature barked excitedly, jumping up and down against the man.

And as the dog jumped, I reached down with a groan—and with both hands, grabbed the dog around the middle.

The dog yipped in surprise as I raised it towards the oven door.

The man uttered a short grunt.

And let go of me.

I dropped to the ground hard, but held on to the pig-man's yapping pet.

"Let us go!" I cried breathlessly. "Let us go—or I'll bake your pet!"

Amy took a step back from the oven, her whole body trembling, her eyes on the dog.

"I'll bake him!" I cried, swinging the squealing pet towards the leaping flames.

The man raised both hands. He backed away. His round, dark eyes were suddenly filled with fear. He kept both hands high, as if in surrender.

Once again, I swung the pet towards the open oven.

The man cried out in protest. He backed up a few more steps.

"Amy—run!" I ordered. "He's going to let us go—as long as he thinks this dog-thing is in danger."

Amy hesitated.

"Run!" I screamed.

She took off, running to the trees.

Still gripping the pet tightly to my chest, I stepped away from the oven. "Don't move!" I shouted to the pig-man. "Don't move! I'll throw him in. I really will!"

The man sighed. His shoulders slumped in defeat.

I backed away another step. Another.

Then I dropped the pet to the ground, spun away, and took off after Amy.

I didn't glance back. I'd never run so fast in my life.

I couldn't breathe. I couldn't see. My legs ached with every step. But I ran . . . ran. . .

I caught up with Amy at the edge of a wide field of corn stalks. "Keep going. . ." I choked out breathlessly. "The stalks will hide us."

"Is he following us?" Amy asked in a tiny voice.

"I don't know," I managed to reply. "I don't think so."

We plunged into the tall, dry stalks. They crackled and swayed as we pushed through them.

After a few minutes, we stopped and dropped to our knees, struggling to catch our breath.

"Now what?" Amy whispered.

I opened my mouth to answer. But a crackling sound near by made me stop.

My heart leaped.

I heard another loud *CRACK*. Scraping footsteps.

So close.

All around us.

The book! I remembered. The end of the *Be Afraid* book flashed back into my mind.

I gazed up at the tall stalks hovering over us. As I stared, they appeared to move, to close in.

"Stelks!" I gasped. "The Stelks—they're coming out of the corn stalks to—to *strangle* us!"

A wave of terror rolled down my body. I shut my eyes.

And heard the dry crunch of footsteps surrounding us.

No time to run. No time to escape.

The tall stalks swayed and bent. Three figures stepped into view.

Three kids about our age! Two boys and a girl. Their mouths opened in shock.

"Huh? Who *are* you?" I choked out.

"Who are *you*?" the girl demanded.

Amy and I stared at them, waiting for them to bare their fangs, spread their wings, reveal their claws.

Were they medieval monsters who prowled this strange land?

"My name is Connor," one of the boys said. "These are my friends, Emily and Kyle."

"No way!" I cried. "I've read *Be Afraid*. I've read the book. You're not real—you're just characters in the book!"

Emily laughed. Kyle, a big, powerful-looking guy, shook his head, frowning.

"We're real," Connor said solemnly. "Here. Pinch my arm."

He held out his arm, and I pinched it. He was real.

"We're not characters," Emily said unhappily. "We're real and we're trapped here. We—"

"Did the wizard send you here?" Kyle interrupted.

Amy squinted at him. "Wizard? We don't know any wizard."

"Then how did you get here?" Connor asked.

"Mark and I started playing the card game," Amy replied. "And as soon as I picked a card, everything went black and—"

"The cards!" Emily cried excitedly. "Did you bring the cards?"

"We need the cards to get home," Connor explained. "Do you have them?"

All three of them stared at us impatiently.

I sighed. "No. I'm sorry. Amy and I searched for the cards. But they are not here. We don't have them."

Connor groaned. "Then we're trapped here."

"We're doomed," Kyle murmured. He grabbed a stalk angrily in both hands and began ripping it apart. "Doomed."

"We don't stand a chance here," Emily said softly. "We're defenceless against all the dragons and evil knights and Krels and Jekels and. . ." Her words caught in her throat. She lowered her eyes to the ground.

"Unless. . ." Amy chimed in.

We all turned to her. "Unless what?" I asked.

"Unless we find another wizard!" Amy stated.

Silence for a long moment.

"Yes! That's brilliant! That's awesome!" Connor declared.

"Yes!" Kyle agreed. "It's a great idea. There *must* be a wizard round here. All the characters from the game are here!"

I laughed. "So we're off to see the wizard?"

We all began singing "Off to See the Wizard", the song from *The Wizard of Oz*, as we made our way through the field of tall corn stalks. Connor and I led the way. I think we were all feeling better. Amy's idea had given us new hope.

We were still singing when we stepped out from the stalks—and stared at an army of Krels, hundreds of them, on horseback, spears and swords drawn, waiting to capture us.

26

I turned. Grabbed Amy. Tried to run back into the corn stalks.

But at least a dozen Krels leaped down off their horses. Before we could move, they had long, jagged daggers pressed to our backs.

"Doomed," Kyle muttered again, shaking his head sadly. "No wizard can help us now."

The Krels marched us across a wide, dark field. They kept their daggers raised and walked close behind us. The rest of the army followed on their horses.

The moon faded behind a grey curtain of clouds. The night air grew cold and wet. My shoes sank and slid in the soft mud.

We marched for hours. My legs ached. My throat felt parched and sore. Sweat ran down my forehead, into my eyes.

Amy was breathing hard, struggling to keep up. "Where are they taking us?" she whispered. "What are they going to do to us?"

I shrugged. "Nothing good," I muttered.

"We're going to walk for ever," Emily complained.

The field ended in a forest of tangled trees and thick bramble bushes. The Krels forced us through the brambles along a narrow, twisting path.

Soon the trees ended and the path led us up a steep, muddy slope.

Behind us, the army of Krels began to chant. *"No mercy... No mercy... No mercy..."*

I swallowed hard. My aching throat throbbed with pain. A sharp pain stabbed my side.

I stopped for a moment, struggling to force away the pain. The tip of a dagger blade in my back forced me to start walking again.

"No mercy... No mercy... No mercy..." The Krels continued their low, ugly chant.

The path curved around the steep slope, then ended.

We stood at the edge of a high cliff. I stared down at the steep drop to the muddy field below.

The Krels raised their daggers. Motioned for us to keep going.

"They're going to force us off the cliff!" Connor cried.

The five of us raised our hands high in surrender.

"Please!" I shouted, trying to be heard over

their steady chant. "Please let us go! We're only kids. We didn't come here to fight you!"

"No mercy. . . No mercy. . . No mercy. . ."

Daggers poised, the Krels moved forward.

We backed up. Backed up until the heels of our shoes poked over the edge of the cliff.

"Goodbye, Mark," Amy said softly, grabbing my hand. "You were a good brother."

I started to choke out a goodbye to her.

But instead I cried, "Hey, wait! I've got an idea!"

I turned to Connor. "Quick—check your shirt pocket."

He squinted at me. "Huh?"

"Hurry!" I cried. "Your shirt pocket. You tucked the wizard card into your pocket!"

"No mercy..." the Krels on horseback chanted. The Krels on foot inched closer to us, their expressions cold and cruel, eyes set menacingly, pointing their dagger blades at our chests.

"How do you know that?" Connor demanded.

"I read it. In the book," I told him. "When the wizard card slid out of the box, you tucked it into your shirt pocket."

Connor's hand shook as he reached into the pocket of his T-shirt—and pulled out the card.

I could see the drawing of Mr Zarwid on it.

"Now what do I do with it?" Connor cried. "How can it help us?"

"Try talking to it!" Emily suggested.

"Huh? It's just a card," Connor protested.

110

"Throw it over the cliff," Kyle suggested. "Maybe that'll send us back home!"

Connor raised his arm. Prepared to throw the card down the steep drop.

"No!" I screamed. "Tear it up, Connor! Tear it to pieces! That will destroy the wizard's magic!"

"Yes! That's it!" Connor cried. He raised the card. Prepared to tear it up.

But a strong gust of wind swirled round us— and blew the card out of his hand, out over the cliff.

"Nooooo!" I uttered a hoarse scream.

Our only hope... Our only hope—floating over the cliff's edge.

Without thinking, I made a wild leap.

My feet flew out from under me.

I grabbed for the card.

Missed.

I heard the kids' screams above me—and real-ized I was falling.

Falling through empty space.

With a last, frantic cry, I swung my hand out as I fell.

And grabbed the wizard card.

Grabbed it—and ripped it.

Ripped it as I plunged down...

Ripped it to pieces.

I saw the ground rising up to meet me.

And then darkness swept over everything.

So dark ... deep and silent.

And cold...

Is it working? I wondered.
Will tearing up the wizard card work?
Will it send us all home?
YOU FINISH THE STORY.

"I don't *believe* this!" I cried. "What a cheat! What a total cheat!"

My friend Brenda lowered her book and frowned across the table at me. "Ross, sshhhh!" She pressed a finger to her lips. "This is supposed to be quiet reading period. You'll get in trouble—"

"I don't care!" I cried. "I'm so angry at this book. It—it—"

"What book?" she whispered, gazing to the front of the class. Our teacher, Miss Freed, had left the room and hadn't returned yet.

"This stupid book I bought at a garage sale," I replied, slamming the book shut. "It's called *Be Afraid*. But it ends right at the good part. It doesn't finish the story."

"Well, why don't you take it back, Ross?" Brenda suggested. "Maybe you can get your money back."

"Good idea," I replied.

Miss Freed had returned. She stood just inside the doorway, frowning at me.

I lowered my eyes to the book and pretended to read.

After school, I decided to take Brenda's advice. I tucked the book into my rucksack and rode my bike to the house down the street where I'd bought it.

Gripping the book tightly under my arm, I rang the doorbell and waited.

A few seconds later, the man who'd run the garage sale pulled open the door. He blinked in the bright sunlight. It took him a while to focus on me.

"I bought this book at your garage sale," I said, holding the book out to him. "But it has no ending. Do you think I could have my money back?"

The man wrinkled his forehead. He gazed down at the book, then at me. "Come in," he said softly. "I think maybe we can make a deal."

"A deal?" I followed him into his cluttered living room.

"I'll make you a trade," the man said, searching through a pile of old books and magazines stacked high on his coffee-table.

He pulled out a small rectangular box and held it out to me. "Try this," he said. A thin smile spread slowly over his wrinkled face. "Some kids have told me that it's a lot of fun."

I took the box and studied it. It was a card game. It was called Be Afraid.

"Looks like fun," I murmured, turning the box over in my hand.

"I've heard it's very exciting," the man replied. "You play it with friends."

"Okay," I agreed. "It's a trade."

I hurried back outside. Tucked the pack of cards into my jacket pocket. And climbed on to my bike.

Then I turned back to the man, who stood watching me from the doorway.

"I'll give it a try!" I called, waving to him. "Thanks a lot, Mr Wardiz!"

Welcome to the new millennium of fear

Check out this chilling preview
of what's next from
R.L. Stine

The Haunted Car

"Bet you ten bucks Mitchell is drawing a car," I heard Allan say from out in the hall.

"No bet," Steve replied. "That's a sucker bet."

They were always betting each other on everything.

They burst into the room and laughed when they saw me hunched over my drawing.

They're both big guys, taller than me and athletic-looking, with broad necks like football players. Allan has curly red hair and a lot of freckles. Mum says he looks like the all-American boy, whatever that means.

Steve has black hair, shaved really short, and wears a silver ring in one ear.

"What are you guys doing here?" I asked, putting down my pen.

"You've been talking non-stop about your awesome new car," Allan replied. "So we came to check it out."

Steve grinned. "You have the keys, Mitchell? You want to take us for a ride?"

"Ha ha," I said, rolling my eyes. "You're a riot."

"You told us your dad let you drive," Steve insisted, picking up my car drawing and studying it.

"Yeah, last summer. But that was way out in the desert in Arizona, and there wasn't another car around for a hundred miles," I replied.

He put the drawing back on the desk and pulled my arm. "Come on. Show us the car."

I led the way to the stairs. Of course, we bumped into Todd. When my friends come over, Todd always manages to be around.

"Where are you going?" he demanded, blocking the stairway.

"To Brazil," Allan joked. "Get out of the way, or we'll miss our plane."

"Take me with you," Todd insisted, crossing his scrawny arms over his scrawny chest.

"Why do you want to go to Brazil?" Allan asked him.

"You're not going to Brazil. You're going to check out the new car," Todd replied.

"Okay, okay, you can come." I sighed. I knew if I didn't agree, he'd come anyway.

I grabbed a jacket and we stepped outside. It was a cool, cloudy night. The ground was still wet from the heavy rains the night before.

Allan and Steve ran past me to the car, which was parked near the bottom of the driveway. Light from the street-lamp poured over it, making the blue finish gleam.

"Way cool!" Allan declared.

Steve ran his hand over the hood, then bent down to examine the headlight covers. "It's built so low," he commented. "Like a racing-car."

"It sounds like a racing-car too," I told him. "It has a V-8 that roars when you floor the accelerator."

"Cool," he murmured. He stood up. "Can we get inside?"

"Yeah. Why not?" I replied.

I grabbed the handle on the driver's side and pulled open the door. The memory of the lock sticking flashed into my mind.

But it hadn't happened again, so I didn't worry about it. Dad probably had everything fixed at the garage.

I slid behind the wheel. Allan climbed in beside me. Todd and Steve piled into the back. We closed all the doors.

"Mmmm. Real leather seats," Steve declared.

"Crank up the radio," Allan demanded.

"I can't," I told him. "I didn't bring the key."

"Well, go and get it," Allan insisted.

"I don't think Dad would like it," I said. "He says if you sit in a car with the radio on, it wears down the battery."

I heard the door locks click.

The sound made me jump.

I turned to Allan beside me. "Did you hit the lock control on your door?"

He shook his head. "No way."

I shivered.

"Hey—it's getting cold in here!" Todd whined. He was right.

I could see my breath steaming towards the windscreen. I shivered again and zipped my jacket up all the way.

I felt a wave of cold air sweep over me. And then another blast, even colder.

"Hey, Mitchell, turn off the AC," Steve called, leaning over the seat. "It's freezing in here."

Shivering, I turned back to him. "The air-conditioning isn't on. I told you, I don't have the key."

"I'm f-f-freezing," Todd stuttered.

I stared at the windscreen. The glass was icing up on the inside!

It's not a normal cold, I realized. It's such a heavy, *deep* cold. Where is it coming from?

"This is totally weird," Allan murmured beside me.

"I'm getting out," Todd declared from behind me. "My face—it's freezing off!"

I heard him tug the door handle. And then I heard him cry out. "Hey—it's locked. Mitchell—unlock the door."

I tried my door. Locked.

Once again, I searched for the lock control.

"It's s-so c-cold!" I heard Steve stammer. "Mitchell—come on. Open the doors."

"I'm trying," I told him. My hand fumbled over the door controls searching for the right button.

The air grew colder. I rubbed my nose and ears. They were numb. My nostrils hurt when I breathed in.

So cold. . .

My chest ached. It suddenly felt tight. I struggled to breathe, but it made my chest throb with pain.

The cold is shutting off my air, I realized. Each breath made a high, wheezing sound.

My chest throbbed. I couldn't stop shivering.

I tried the door again. But my numb fingers wouldn't bend. I couldn't grab the handle.

Frantic, choked with panic, I shoved my shoulder against it. No.

It wouldn't budge.

And then I heard laughter. Very faint. A girl's laughter. Soft and . . . cruel.

Mean laughter.

The air grew even colder. I choked. Struggled to draw in a breath. But I couldn't.

Had my lungs frozen?

"Let us out!" Todd shrieked.

"Let us out of here!" Steve screamed.

We were all pounding on the doors and windows.

"Let us out! Somebody—let us out!"